T0164761

THE
SENATOR

By

Dr. Carl R. Stekelenburg

Order this book online at www.trafford.com
or email orders@trafford.com

Most Trafford titles are also available at major online book retailers.

Printed in the United States of America.

ISBN: 978-1-4269-9273-5 (sc)
ISBN: 978-1-4269-9274-2 (e)

Trafford rev. 08/23/2011

 www.trafford.com

North America & international
toll-free: 1 888 232 4444 (USA & Canada)
phone: 250 383 6864 ♦ fax: 812 355 4082

DEDICATION

This is my sixth book and I wish to thank many people whom I have thanked personally, but not in print: My brother John has served as technical advisor over many of my books, several typists have typed my books. These included Diane McCommel, Patsy Manning, and Hannah Butts. All typists have also helped me with editing, as I am blind. Additionally friends have helped. These include, but are not limited to, Amber Howard, Nancy Freeman, Brenda Freeman, and my mother Elma Stekelenburg.

A variety of people have helped in a variety of ways with advice. Not everyone has helped on every book. The final decision to publish was mine alone and none of the above are to be blamed for the final manuscript as I am responsible.

Dr. Carl R. Stekelenburg
LaGrange, GA
August 2011

DISCLAIMER

This is a work of fiction. No persons or events are true or actual. While historical characters may appear, any resemblance to a person living or dead is purely coincidental and a product of the author's imagination.

ABOUT THE AUTHOR

Dr. Carl R. Stekelenburg is a single man, blinded in 1993 in a mistaken identity attack. He was reared in the Midwest having lived in Minnesota, Iowa, Missouri, Oklahoma, and Texas. Following graduation from college in Oklahoma, he served in the United States Air Force stateside during the Vietnam War. After his military service, he was an educator and administrator in Florida and Georgia. Upon completion of his doctorate in education at the University of Georgia in 1991, he was hired as

Superintendent of Schools for Charlton County in Folkston, Georgia, where he was attacked and clubbed blind in 1993. Previously he served as Superintendent of Meriwether County Schools for seven years during the 1980's. He is the father of two daughters, Tammy and Jenny.

Dr. Stekelenburg is the author of five previous books, "The Burton Murder and Other Short Stories", "Blind Date", "High Plains Cowboy", "Gunfight at Dutchman's Well", and "Canadian Cowgirl".

He now resides in Lagrange, Georgia. After eighteen years of blindness, he continues to enjoy books on tape from the Library of Congress and authoring novels.

"The Senator" is his sixth book.

PROLOGUE

Officer Robert Williams gets his Master's Degree in Criminal Justice and is quickly promoted from road duties to command duties with a rank of Captain. He is placed in command of the Waycross, Georgia patrol post.

His assistant is Ron Astro. Ron's wife is Dr. Linda Astro, professor of political science at Waycross College. Governor Nathan Deal had the responsibility of appointing a new U.S. Senator upon the death by heart attack of the existing junior senator. Officers Ron and Robert had both performed courteous service for the governor and his protection detail on his visits to Waycross.

The previous year they and their wives, Dr. Linda and Penny, had attended a governor's ball and fundraising dinner at Waycross College. The governor had been impressed with both couples. He was particularly impressed with the economic and political understanding of both Dr. Linda and Robert.

When the junior senator died of a heart attack, the governor, already acquainted with Dr. Linda Astro, quickly appointed her to fill the remaining term of that senator as provided by state law. Linda quickly accepted, but didn't mention she was three weeks pregnant. Off to Washington D.C. she went. She represented Georgia quite well, but the child continued to grow within her. Soon she was forced to seek maternity leave. Governor Deal had to appoint someone on a temporary basis while Dr. Linda was in the hospital. This was just too important a time for Georgia not to have two senators in Washington. President Obama was pushing for an increase in the debt ceiling for the current budget year of 2011. He had already shoved down Georgia's throat the Obama health care plan. Governor Deal immediately thought of Officer Williams to fill the post temporarily while Dr. Linda was in the hospital.

Officer Williams requested and was granted extended leave without pay to temporarily become a U.S. Senator.

This book is his story.

CHAPTER 1

In the year 2011, a Georgia highway patrol captain got his Master's Degree in criminal justice at a young age. His name was Robert Williams. He had just been promoted to captain, but had not yet been assigned as commander of his own Georgia highway control post. He is still out on patrol in his own brand new 2012 Ford Taurus Police Interceptor. His car was equipped with all the goodies including AWD EcoBoost 3.5 liter twin turbo model with 365hp, a radar based monitoring system that alerts for cross traffic, blind spot obstacles, and a rear radar chimes for safety. Also included is a ballistic door insert to protect against gunfire, a shotgun rack, a radar gun, and a MacBook for checking outstanding warrants and other information.

The only downside that Robert could tell was the backseat space. With the new Lexan bulletproof divider, the backseat was a little cramped for prisoner transport. There are no inside door handles or window controls for the prisoners to get out, without an officer opening the door from the outside. Robert was proud of this new V6 Interceptor, which far out paced his old LTD V8. In addition, he liked the AWD, which allowed him to turn around in the interstate medians and pursue a car speeding in the other direction.

Having not received his promotion command yet, Robert was on traffic control service on this day. As he sat to the left of the interstate, facing north at the median, a speeding red Impala travelling south at high speed blew by with what looked like a six-pack of college girls headed to the beach. Robert dropped the transmission of his Ford Interceptor into drive, cut the wheels left and adroitly spun the wheel and headed south. As the grass was wet from the previous evening shower, the all wheel drive transmission worked great to get him across the median of HWY US1. Captain Williams punched the Interceptor's 365hp V6 super high output engine into action. In no time he pulled up next to the Impala and signaled them to pull over. His red and blue thin light bar was flashing rapidly a mile ahead. Driver of the Impala, Suzanne Brooks, eased the Impala to a stop at the right hand side of the road in the emergency lane. Captain Williams also got on the binders and pulled smoothly in behind the Impala. On his public address system he ordered the driver to pull the car farther to the right, so when he walked up to the door he would not get struck by passing traffic.

First Robert engaged his MacBook to check for outstanding warrants on the tag number. Finding none he exited the Taurus and adjusted his service weapon on his hip. He was carrying the standard issue Glock. The Captain didn't think he would need it, as this looked like six high-spirited college girls. As Robert approached the left rear of the red Impala, he again noticed six heads where only five should be. He determined to give these college girls a good scolding. Obviously, one was not wearing a seat belt in this five-passenger vehicle. As he approached the driver's door, he politely asked for the driver's Georgia driver's license. The car was carrying Muscogee County, Georgia plates.

Suzanne reached nervously into her purse and handed him a laminated card. This turned out to be her work I.D. as a Muscogee County librarian. Officer Williams responded, "That may get you in the library, but it won't allow you to drive on the road."

"Sorry, officer, I'm so nervous I was distracted." Next, she handed him a laminated card, which said, 'Georgia Forestry Smoke Jumper'. Robert replied, "That won't do either, do you think you're on your way to a fire?"

"Yes sir! I'm a certified smoke jumper and I'm on my way to a raging forest fire at the Okefenokee Swamp. The fire has been burning down there for months now, but a nursing home is in danger now. Several of us qualified smoke jumpers have been called in on an emergency basis."

Robert responded, "Are all six of you ladies smoke jumpers?"

The lady in the right front seat was bending over while trying to light something. Robert wondered if it was a marijuana cigarette. He asked, "What is your name and what are you doing?"

The lady responded, "My name is Alisa, and I'm lighting a Marlboro, if it's any of your business. You see I'm nervous and I smoke when I'm nervous. And no I'm not a smoke jumper, but I am a smoke inhaler."

He responded as she inhaled deeply. Next, she began a coughing spasm.

Captain Williams was an extreme proponent of non-smoking. So, he responded, "Those cancer sticks are going to kill you and your five friends if you're not careful. Plus, with everything so dry right now, you'd be setting the grass along this highway on fire. We don't need that!"

Then turning to Suzanne he said, "First of all you haven't shown me your driver's license and secondly you were speeding and lastly, you are driving with six passenger in a five passenger vehicle. One of the ladies in the back is obviously not wearing a seat belt. You may be going to a fire to save some lives, but what worries me is how many lives you'd be taking along the way."

Suzanne finally located her driver's license, which she now handed to the angry officer. Officer Williams continued writing the ticket recording the license name and number before returning the laminated card to Suzanne. Then he turned to the four ladies in the back seat saying, "Please identify yourselves. Are you all smoke jumpers?"

All four responded, "No way, we are all college students on the way to Daytona Beach." Kay, took the lead and said, "We are all bankers. To my right is Dianne, to her right are Tennalla and Brenda, respectively."

That really set Robert's face a flame. He was already nearly at his wits end with these college kids. So he asked, "So are you the very bankers who have caused the mortgage crisis in America by making home loans to people who really can't pay them back?"

All five ladies blushed and shook their heads no. Just then the public address horn on Robert's Taurus Interceptor barked out, "Officer Williams, we have been trying to reach you. Please respond so we may know you're O.K."

Robert reached up on his shoulder mic and squeezed the transmit button. And he said, "Robert here. I'm just fine but frustrated with a six pack of college girls."

Both his car speaker and the speaker on his shoulder responded with, "We think you are working the radar on US1, south of Waycross. If so, there has been a prison bus stolen by two prisoners who are working fire suppression at the Okefenokee Swamp. They overpowered a guard who was giving first aid to one of them, then took his bus keys and escaped. Be careful, the officer's side arm is missing. Please consider them armed and dangerous, my love."

Robert grinned to himself. He knew his wife, Penny, was the dispatcher on duty, so he decided to correct her radio procedure, saying, "If this is my wife speaking, then brush up on your radio procedure. As the new commander to be and about to be wearing railroad track bars, I will need to be enforcing proper radio procedure." Then falling out of radio procedure himself, he said, "Sorry, honey, I didn't mean to be sharp with you. But, with the new responsibilities will come additional pressures! Oh! Oh! I see that prison van headed north now." Robert finished speaking into his shoulder mic then turned to Suzanne at the driver's wheel and said, "Stay put. I'll be right back."

He hot footed it back to his Interceptor and entered the air-conditioned space. The cool air sure felt great. He quickly engaged the drive lever and after checking carefully for oncoming traffic both ways, he spun the wheel across the US1 median and fell in right behind the slow moving grey prison bus. Marked in black letters on the bus was 'D. Ray James Prison Folkston, Georgia'.

With the blue and red lights flashing on his thin light bar, he engaged his loud speaker, "Prisoners, immediately pull that prison van to the side of the road." His deep voice boomed over the loud speaker. Toby Howard was behind the wheel and immediately complied. Just then, his police radio came back to life. Knowing Penny's voice he heard, "Officer Williams," then he said in a very proper police voice, "The escaped prisoners have been identified as Tim Payne and Toby Howard. Both are in prison for felony possession of weapons."

Officer Williams stopped the Taurus, let the engine run for the air conditioning to continue, placed the transmission in park, set the parking break, and pulled his 12 gauge shotgun from his center mounted vertical rack. As he exited the vehicle, he kept his body behind the special bullet protective shield of his door. As he stood to his full 6'2" height, the 250 pound officer easily pumped a 12 gauge buckshot shell into the firing chamber with his left hand, while he lifted the shotgun into firing position with his right hand. Deciding to take no chances of the prisoners pulling away in the prison bus as he approached, officer Williams discharged a full load of buckshot's into the tires on the left dual wheel. Quickly jacking another shell into the chamber, he dispatched the right two tires also. Then pumping a third shell into the firing chamber, officer Williams pushed the door closed on his Interceptor with his right knee to preserve the air-conditioned space. He leveled the 12-gauge shotgun with both hands and shouted loudly, "Hands behind your heads." Then he walked slowly up to the left side of the prison bus. With shotgun leveled at Toby Howards head, he commanded, "Out of the vehicle and face down on the pavement." When Toby Howard complied, he ordered Tim Payne to join him saying, "Payne, you cross in front of the bus and join Howard on the ground." Payne thought about pulling the service revolver from his waist band that he had taken from the guard, but looking down the barrel of that 12-guage, he decided to leave his hands behind his hand. He complied with the orders of the officer and went prone with his head next to Howard's feet.

Officer Williams called in for back up on his shoulder mic. As Tim Payne lay prone, Robert observed the guard's revolver still stuck behind the prisoner's belt. Placing his shotgun barrel at the back of Payne's head, he decided it was safe to reach for the weapon with his left hand, which he did. Backing away towards his patrol car, Officer Williams decided to wait for further back up.

With Penny at the dispatcher's microphone, three other cruisers soon assembled along HWY1 north. Williams quickly brought them up to date and then returned to the waiting Impala. By the time he arrived back at the Impala in the southbound lane, the hot South Georgia sun had caused the college girls to raise the white fabric roof on the convertible. Now behind the red Impala was a red 2002, 55' T-Bird remake. Its white convertible top was also in the up position. Apparently both drivers wisely were seeking shelter from the hot South Georgia sun. Williams spoke into his public address microphone, "T-Bird driver, exit your vehicle, walk behind the vehicle, and stand with your hands on the trunk." A red haired good-looking female complied promptly. As she approached the trunk of her car, she placed her hands on the trunk where they were burned on the hot re painted metal. She quickly jerked them back and complained, "Officer, I'll hold my hands in the air, but that trunk is just too hot to hold." And then she extended her arms upward.

Williams pressed the speak button on his public address microphone and he said, "Sorry. I didn't realize how hot your car was. Dressed in the outfit you are wearing, I can see that you are not armed. You may lower your hands." He placed the microphone back on the dashboard and exited the vehicle. He did place his right hand on his service Glock, however. With his left hand on the driver's door he closed it while keeping his right hand on the service Glock. He was a little up tight from his recent encounter with Payne and Howard. Staring ahead at this very attractive middle aged red haired woman, he secretly admired her trim figure and expensive looking slacks. Seeing those form fitting clothes, he knew she possessed no weapon, so he removed his hand from his service weapon.

He asked, "Who are you? And are you with the red Impala, too?"

The beautiful lady replied, "My name is Dr. Joanne Crimson. I have been called to the Okefenokee Swamp to administer to an injured prison officer. My office is in Waycross so I was heading south to Folkston when I saw the stopped red Impala belonging to my friend and librarian, Suzanne Brooks. I just stopped to say, 'Hello,' is that O.K. Officer?"

Robert, embarrassed, thought, "This day has really been a tough one." Then he responded, "Doctor, go ahead and re-enter your vehicle and proceed to the treatment of the downed officer." So Joanne re-entered the T-Bird and sped away.

Officer Williams cautiously returned to the red Impala. He tapped lightly on the driver's window and Suzanne lowered the power window. Still wearing a single bar on each shoulder of his uniform, the soon to be Captain Williams said,

"It's just too hot to stand out here in the sun and discuss your ticket with this many offenses. Let's all adjourn to that Denny's restaurant immediately ahead. Pull in there and we will discuss how you will proceed with your overloaded vehicle."

This they did. And over cold iced tea in the Denny's booth, Robert explained why they could not drive on Georgia public roads without a seatbelt for every passenger. He suggested, "If the smoke jumper, Suzanne, needs to get to the swamp, and one of you is a licensed driver to drive her car, I will take Ms. Suzanne in my patrol car and get her quickly to her mission. I guess, I'll issue a warning ticket since your driver was headed to a true emergency."

Robert and Suzanne travelled even faster than she was flying in the Impala. With lights ablaze and sirens blasting they sped down to the North Charlton County entrance of the Okefenokee Swamp.

On the way, Suzanne explained, "Most people don't associate 'librarians' with 'smoke jumpers'. However, I've been a member of the skydiving club in Waycross for forty years. When I moved here from South Carolina to become head librarian at the Ware County library, the forestry service had me listed as a certified parachutist and asked me would I be willing to serve on a volunteer basis in an emergency. I thought 'diving into the swamp' would be exciting, so I agreed." Leaving Suzanne at the forest service fire truck, Robert turned his Taurus in a tight U-turn and headed back to US1 and the situation at the prison bus.

After issuing instructions to his fellow patrolmen, Robert returned to the Waycross post and the officers took the prisoners back to D. Ray James Prison. When he arrived at the patrol post, Ron approached him in an excited manner. He said, "Let's go in your office, please, Robert." Inside the office behind a closed door, Ron explained to Robert that his wife, Senator Linda Astro, was about to give birth immanently. He further explained that Governor Deal had been trying to get in touch with Robert to fill the position temporarily. Robert excused himself and walked up to the dispatch desk where he discussed the situation with Penny. She quickly agreed that he should take the position and Robert requested her to call the governor's office and transfer the call to his office. Upon re-entering his office and taking a seat, the phone immediately rang. As Robert picked up the phone receiver, he heard, "Please hold for Governor Deal."

Governor Deal's voice came on the line, "Robert, Senator Astro is going out on emergency leave, and this is just too important a time in Washington to be without second senatorial vote. I need you to go to Washington D.C. within 48 hours to be ready on the floor of the Senate at that time. Please call Dr. Astro to bring you up to date on the current situation. Will you be willing to serve as temporary senator?"

Robert replied, "Certainly, Governor Deal. I would consider it a privilege. I know that your position on Obama Care and national debt agree with Senator Astro and mine, so we will all be in accord without problem."

They hung up and Robert decided to drive his Ford F150 pick up to Washington D.C. so he would have to hustle. He wanted to carry a firearm, as is required of all off duty police officers. The reason for this is former convicted felons, once released, and could seek revenge against the arresting officer. Robert had decided to carry his ankle holster and small revolver, as he knew D.C. was the murder capital of the country. There were more murders in D.C. per thousand citizens, than anywhere in the country. He planned to go armed. Flying could be arranged, but the permit process would take more than 48 hours. Mailing the revolver would take more than 48 hours, too. So, Robert decided to drive his Ford F150 pickup to D.C. He quickly entered his patrol car and sped home with lights ablaze. When he reached Folkston, he turned onto the whelp portion of his siren. He came to a stop to the right of his pickup parking his patrol car on the grass by his driveway.

In minutes, two suitcases were jammed full of his dress clothes, one being a suit bag and the other a bag on rollers containing his undergarments. Strapping the ankle-holstered gun on, he jumped in the F150 and departed. He noted that his emergency red flasher light was still perched in the center of the dashboard behind the windshield. The wire connecting the power to the battery was plugged into his cigarette lighter. It had a toggle switch that he could easily reach with his thumb. In Robert's shirt pocket was a highway patrol I.D. On the seat beside him was the governor's commission as US Senator.

As Robert entered the flow of traffic down US1 connecting him to HWY 40 east and then to I-95 north, he used his red light only when necessary. His mind was thinking back to leaving the command of the Waycross post with Ron and everyone calling him "Senator" in a joking but pleased fashion.

Proceeding north through South Carolina, North Carolina, and Virginia, he arrived in D.C. ahead of schedule.

Securing a room at the Watergate Hotel, he quickly changed from patrol uniform to grey dress slacks and navy blazer. A striped red, white, and blue tie completed the outfit. Marching resolutely with commission in hand and service revolver strapped to his ankle and patrol officer's ID in his coat pocket, he proceeded to the senate "Sgt. At Arms" office.

Sgt. At Arms, being a former secret service agent was alert to the bulge at his ankle. He said, "Senator Williams, I know you are a highway patrolman Captain back in Georgia. However, you will not be allowed on the Senate floor with that pistol strapped to your ankle. If you'll surrender that weapon to me at this time, I'll return it to you as you leave the chamber later. Thank you." Robert surrendered his weapon without complaint.

His paperwork being in order, he was admitted to his desk on the Senate floor. The Sgt. Of Arms further handed him a key and the room number of his office in the 'rustle senate office building'.

By that afternoon, Vice President Joe Biden was recognizing Senator Williams as a new junior senator from Georgia. The swearing in ceremony lasted only a minute. His fellow senator's applauded politely. He noticed that republicans applauded just a little bit longer and louder than the democrats.

Later that evening, as the senate worked late into the night on President Obama's budget request to increase the national debt before August 2, 2011, Senator Williams cast his first 'No' vote of his career.

Suddenly, an angry voice was heard in the back of the chamber. Rushing down the aisle was a disabled Army retiree from the special forces shouting, "All the months of danger and injury that I had in my three deployments to Iraq, I think I deserve more than I'm getting in my retirement check. I've lost most of my ability to work, and now you're talking about no pay for injured soldiers. I bet on August 2nd, you senators pay yourself while threatening to cut benefits from disabled veterans!" The angry retired Sergeant waved his pistol in the air. Senator Williams wished now that the Sgt. At Arms had not taken his ankle weapon, yet the angry disabled veteran was distracted by watching the secret service drag Vice President Biden out the back door to safety. As the Sergeants eyes were glazed forward, the new Senator launched himself at his back. He pulled his arms around his chest and pulled both arms down. The injured special forces Sergeant was unable to lift his arms or fire his gun as Senator Williams' weight forced him down to the floor of the Senate. As Senator Williams, 250 pounds forced a breath from the struggling man, another Senator, a veteran of the Korean War, quickly placed his foot on the gun of the irate man. Bending down, the Senator from North Carolina quickly removed the weapon and lowered the hammer safely. Capital police called by the Sgt. At Arms quickly took the situation under their control and removed him from the Senate. The Senators resumed their seats and debate proceeded.

As Robert Williams sat in his chair on the Senate floor, his mind drifted to his son Dusty. He was glad that Dusty had been such a good student and person that such behavior, as just exhibited on the Senate floor, would not be characteristic of Dusty.

In fact, Robert could only think of one problem he had with Dusty. Dusty had become enamored with a pretty young girl who was dating a Future Farmers of America (FFA) Student. Dusty had been a football player and involved in college bound courses. Dusty had no knowledge of agriculture or farming or horses for that matter but, because he wanted to impress this young lady, Gail he rented a horse. Gail watched Dusty try to step into the saddle to show off for her. But, being inexperience, he forgot to tighten the girth properly. The saddle slid and deposited Dusty on the hard ground. Gail responded with a shout. The horse became even more startled, jerked away with his reins dragging to one side. Holding his to one side, he avoided stepping on the dragging reins. He plunged across four lanes of US 1, nearly causing a collision in both directions. Embarrassed, Dusty began following the horse to catch his reins. As they proceeded along the road into the federal wildlife preserve, Okefenokee Swamp, every time Dusty approached the horse he would jog off ahead of him then stop and wait for him. Dusty began to approach from behind; the horse repeated this same procedure over and over. Finally exhausted and sweating, Dusty looked around for an answer. Just then Gail pulled up in her old Toyota pick up. She lowered the window on Dusty's side and said, "Climb in, Dusty, you've got to approach that horse from the front. I'll drive you around." So she did. Once Dusty exited the pick up and approached the horse from the front he stood calmly still and waited on him. Dusty grabbed the reins, checked the girth, lifted the reins around the neck of the animal and rode safely back to the rental barn. Gail had not been very impressed. Suddenly, Senator Williams was elbowed by the senior Senator from Georgia and he had to quit his daydreaming.

As the evening wore on, Robert grew more self-confident. When finally recognized by Vice President Biden, Robert rose to speak.

"Mr. Vice President, fellow senators, and members of the press floor, I'm senator Williams, junior senator from Georgia on my first full day in US Senate. That doesn't mean I haven't been thinking about these issues for a very long time. It's my understanding that we now spend about 40% of all federal revenues to pay the interest on the national debt. Pshaw, my old daddy was smart enough to know that you can't spend more than you take in. In fact, we old Georgia boys know your money must work for you, instead of you working for your money. As the richest nation on Earth, we need to be loaning money at interest, not borrowing it at interest. I read in the newspapers that we currently give foreign aid to about 50 countries around the world. Why are we doing this? You can't buy friendship. Most of these countries don't even like us, yet we borrow money to give it to them? Now I'm not a politician, I'm a police officer, but I'm smart enough to know that's not good business."

The junior senator from Georgia, Robert Williams, then continued, "Mr. Obama wants us to raise the debt ceiling again. I say vote 'No'. It's time to stop this insanity."

"I have a budget at my house that I must live within or go bankrupt. I'm probably the only man in the senate, today, who is not a millionaire. I'm also probably the only one who's not in personal debt. As I will be in my hotel room tonight, I will use my MacBook to prepare each of you a family budget. This is what your constituents have to do every month. Also, please realize that about 10% of all your constituents don't have a job right now. With no income, except maybe some unemployment insurance they must do some serious trimming of their budget. We must do the same as their elected representatives. Our state constitution in Georgia requires that we not spend more than we take in annually."

At that time there was a round of applause from some republican senators and some guests in the upper visitor's gallery.

Senator Williams continued, "Tonight I will prepare a budget sheet for a typical family. The median income for a family of four in this country is about $44,000 a year. Please work out a budget with $3,600 a month. First deduct about half of that in taxes and medical insurance. Start with a cash income of $1,800 a month. As millionaires, you don't realize how hard it is for the average family to feed and cloth two children, send them to school, provide transportation, and housing. Speaking of housing, the foreclosure rate in this country is approaching 10%. This is partially because bankers are issuing questionable loans where the purchaser has little hope of repaying them. Foreclosures are the understandable result.

"We must stop shipping our jobs overseas. There should be no tax breaks for companies producing their goods offshore with cheap labor. The tax code needs to be simplified. Breaks for the rich either reduced or eliminated.

"We need to stop spending half of this world's total expenditure on military equipment and personnel. President Obama has been given the Nobel Peace Prize, yet now we are fighting five wars at one time in the Middle East. We've been in Afghanistan more than ten years. Our longest war ever. The Soviets fought there for ten years and then left and now we've jumped in for ten years. It's time we've left. We cannot force our style of democracy on people who have lived in a tribal society for thousands of years. They neither want nor understand it.

"One of the best things that can happen to a country it appears, is to lose a war to the United States. More than sixty years after WWII, we still have troops in Germany and Japan. Now we buy their cars and have a balance of trade deficit with them.

"We need to bring the troops home. These wars are costing us more than 2 billion dollars a week. We need to spend that money on infrastructure here at home. Our electrical grid is old and needs updating as evidenced by the recent Brown Out in the Northeast from Ohio to New York. The electrical grid collapsed in a domino effect. Our railroads have not been maintained, and may now be the worst in the world for public transportation. Our interstates and federal highways need to be upgraded. The bridges are getting old and cracked. Our priorities are in the wrong places."

The senator next to Williams was the senior senator from Georgia. He tapped him on the pocket of his sports jacket. Robert took this as a clue that he was getting too long winded.

Taking the hint, Senator Williams commented, "I now yield the remainder of my time to the senior senator from Georgia." With that, Georgia's newest senator sat down.

Upon return to the Watergate, Senator Robert prepared the following blank form for his colleagues in the senate to see what their typical constituents had to face trying to provide for a family of four for $1,600 a month.

FAMILY EXPENDITURES

AT SIXTEEN HUNDRED MONTHLY

FOOD

CLOTHING

SHELTER
     HOUSE PAYMENT

TAXES

INSURANCE

UTILITIES
     ELECTRICITY
     WATER AND SEWAGE

TRANSPORTATION
     CAR PAYMENT
     CAR INSURANCE
     FUEL
     REPAIRS
     PUBLIC TRANSPORTATION

CHARITIES AND GIFTS
     CHURCH
     FAMILY AND FRIENDS
     CHARITIES

FAMILY EXPENDITURES

AT SIXTEEN HUNDRED MONTHLY

MEDICAL COST
    HEALTH INSURANCE
    MEDICINE
    DR. VISIT
    DENTIST
    OPTOMERTIST
    OTHER

COMMUNICATION

    TELEPHONE
    INTERNET
    NEWSPAPER
    CABLE TELEVISION
    POSTAGE
    OTHER

TOTAL MONTHLY EXPENDITURES

_____

The previous form was distributed to every senator's mailbox the following morning.

When Joe Biden resumed the chair in the senate chamber, early the next morning, he noticed that Senator Williams' budget form was on top of his 'in' tray. This reminded him that they had adjourned the previous day while the senior senator from Georgia had the floor. Debate had been postponed. So after the opening formalities he said, "The senior senator from Georgia has the floor. Mr. Senator, you have the floor."

The senior senator rose and said, "My colleague Senator Williams had loaned me the balance of his time. I now yield it back to Senator Williams."

Robert stood up and said, "Thank you senator. To complete my arguments I wish to speak about our social security system, infrastructure repair suggestions, and the need to stop policing the whole world.

"First of all, our 300 million people are only about 6% of the world's population. Yet, we think we need to police the other 94% of the world. I don't think this is wise or sustainable. We need to stop spending half of the world's military expenditure.

"Our senior citizens have been told that the cost of living has not gone up in the past three years. They deserve a raise. We all know the cost of living has gone up. The problem is, there is no social security 'trust fund'. Back when Harry Truman was president and social security payments started in 1946, the then current retirees retirement was paid by the then working men and women. Politicians in election after election have talked about preserving the 'social security trust fund/lock box'. This is an illusion. This government borrows and spends the social security total amount received from employers every year. They forward the employee's 6.5% of pay and their own matching 6.5%. This 13% is capped at $85,000. When Tiger Woods or some other professional athlete receives $20 million or more per year in income, we need to tax that full amount. When prize money is handed out at Augusta, Georgia, the sponsor needs to forward the total 13%, half from the golf course and half from the winner. As rich employers don't wish to pay the matching 6.5%, they have pressured you for a low cap on social security payments. If the rich businessmen haven't bought your vote, then you need to solve the social security income/pay out problem. Then we can have enough money to give our seniors all of their COLA (Cost of Living Adjustment). We need to stop borrowing their money at no interest to fund our five wars overseas. We need to stop spending about $2 billion a week dropping bombs in the Middle East and spend that money back at home fixing up the country. Instead of destroyers, let's be builders.

"On the question of infrastructure, I would like to see a modern monorail public transportation system built down the center of our interstate highway system. We also could add connecting branches too. Another idea would be to add mass transit monorail where needed in our major cities.

"Let me speak now about our dwindling oil supply world wide. In this country, we purchase and burn about half of the world's oil. Oil discoveries are not keeping pace. In addition, other industrialized nations and the third world countries all want their cars, too. Oil prices are being driven up by not only China and India, with a huge population, but also by our greedy oil company executives. Gas prices are at an all time high along with profits for the oil company. Why not support industry efforts for the development of a hydrogen/fuel cell car. These cars run on electricity generated by H2O or water and oxygen. Fuel would cost nearly nothing. But, naturally oil company executives don't want this. I hope the oil companies don't have your vote in their pockets, due to you accepting their campaign contributions."

Several senators began squirming in their seats. Many owned shares in major oil companies.

"Lastly, for today," Robert chuckled, "We need to allow stem cell research for medical cures. This does not mean killing babies in the womb. Stem cells are available from teeth roots and blood from the umbilical cord, which will be thrown away anyhow. These stem cells may hold a solution to many of our medical challenges.

"We need to find alternative sources of energy, other than just oil. For example, solar power and wind power to generate electricity. Also, the burning of garbage for electrical production may help solve our garbage dump problem, too.

"I will prepare another paper for you over night. This form will contain a typical family's saving plan, so that when they reach retirement age, 'their money can work for them instead of them working for money'. I would appreciate your understanding of how non-senators have to struggle to save for their retirement years. Their wealth typically will not have been handed down from generation to generation. We need to look seriously at a cap on tax-free transfer of extreme wealth from generation to generation. For example, a tenth generation multimillionaire family has no incentive to work. Work is important to self-esteem. Now that I've stepped on every one of your toes, I guess I'll sit down." Robert smiled.

As the senate day ended, Robert returned to the Watergate and developed the following saving's form.

FAMILY EXPENDITURES

AT SIXTEEN HUNDRED MONTHLY

FAMILY SAVINGS
    BANKS
        PASSBOOK SAVINGS
        CERTIFICATES OF DEPOSIT
        MONEY MARKETS
        U.S. SAVINGS BONDS

MUTUAL FUNDS

ANNUITIES

REAL ESTATE
    HOME
    RENTAL PROPERTIES

BUSINESS
    OTHER

COLLECTIBLES
    GOLD
    COINS
    OTHER

TOTAL_____

The following morning, these printouts of a family saving's plan were distributed in the senator's mailboxes. Again, when Vice President Biden took his seat, Senator Williams' document was on the top of his 'in' box. After the opening ceremonies, Vice President Biden said, "Does everyone have Senator Williams' document this morning? For a freshman senator, Mr. Williams seems to have caught fire. I'll ask him to discuss this briefly. Senator Williams you have the floor."

Senator Williams stood up and started, "Thank you Mr. Vice President, I just want all of the rich senators to understand how difficult savings is for a low paying job. Yet, they have the same needs as everyone else. Sudden emergencies, such as loss of a job or health issues, can be a real strain on their budget and savings plan.

"The congress, republicans and democrats alike, have continued to grow this government. We work for the people, but many bureaucrats and elected representatives think that the people work for us. Washington has creeped the percentage of the gross national product that's meant for taxes, to about one third of all gross national product. Economists like your regular junior Georgia senator, Dr. Linda Astro, warn that we can never approach 50% of gross national product being consumed by the government and avoid a total economic collapse. It is simply unsustainable. We are rapidly approaching that point. My Taurus Interceptor back in Georgia, where I actually work for a living, has anti-lock brakes. We need some kind of anti-lock brake system installed for congress's spending. We may need to pass a 'balance budget amendment' to the US constitution.

"My fellow senators, you have a mighty stressful and important job here. It's not my cup of tea, however. My cup of tea may be the tea party's position." Robert chuckled, and then continued, "I can't wait for Dr. Linda to get her health back and deal with these stresses. I want to go home to the 'safe' Georgia highway patrolman job." Robert smiled and sat down.

At the conclusion of the Senate day, Senator Williams stopped by the Sgt. Of Arms desk and restraped his ankle holster on and exited the building. He had left his Ford F150 in the parking garage at the Watergate Hotel. Rather than calling a taxi, Robert decided to walk past the mall back to the Watergate. As he past the Korean War Memorial, he sat down on the bench to catch his breath. As he read the inscriptions on the war memorial, he was approached by three black youths. The first one was obviously the leader. He said, "We followed you from the Senate building. Obviously you're a rich Senator and we want your billfold." Next the young man reached into his right pants pocket and produced a switchblade knife. He depressed the button and the blade flipped out.

Seeing the switchblade knife, Senator Williams reached to his ankle holster and removed his weapon. It was a small .32 caliber revolver. The senator said, "Why did you bring a knife to a gun fight? It may surprise you to learn that I'm on

Senate security force, rather than a rich senator." Robert told a little white lie.

All three young men stared with wide eyes at the barrel of that weapon. The youth with the switchblade was so startled he dropped the knife. It hit the concrete walk with a resounding "clang". Robert first reached to his shoulder mic, but realized he wasn't wearing his highway patrol uniform. Recovering rapidly, he reached to his inside pocket and located his cell phone. Flipping it open with his thumb he punched in 911 left handed. He told the operated his location and requested assistance. D.C. police promptly arrived and after hearing the Senator's story, placed the three young black men in the back of a patrol car and departed for the police station.

Meanwhile, Robert had replaced the gun in his ankle holster and hid it underneath his pants leg. He departed for the Watergate and his hotel room. There he prepared his speech for the next Senate meeting. He reviewed the fact that people on Social Security had not received a Cost of Living Adjustment (COLA) in three years. This non-inflation figure had been computed by the Congressional Budget office. Representative Lynn Westmoreland of Newnan, Georgia had consulted previously with the new senator. Congressman Westmoreland informed Senator Williams that members of Congress had similarly not received a COLA for three years either. Not that Senator Williams was concerned about his senatorial salary, but this was ridiculous. Where had those Congressional budget staffers been? He thought, "Had they not been to the grocery store, paid their light bill, or been to the doctor lately?"

Next Robert flipped on his television to CNN news. The reporter announced the death of 36 American service personnel in Afghanistan. Their twin rotor, heavy lift, helicopter had been shot down by an RPG or rocket propelled grenade. It was the deadliest day for American troops in the ten years of the Afghanistan war. Robert agreed with 70% of the American public, who thought it was time to get out of Afghanistan.

Like millions of Americans, Robert failed to see what was being accomplished there. He mused, "These people have lived in tribal structure society and have been fighting for thousands of years in those caves and rocks. They neither understand nor want western style democracy. The Russians fought there for 10 years and now we've fought there for 10 years. What has been accomplished?"

Looking back on world history, Robert realized that the Colonial Period of domination of countries around the world by European powers had been unsuccessful. He knew that England could not control the United States back in 1776. Likewise they had to give up India and return Hong Kong to China in 1997. It was time to realize that we Americans were only 6% of the world's population. How could we be policeman to the other 94%?

The next morning back at the Capital building, Senator Williams again checked his ankle holstered weapon with the Sgt. Of Arms and proceeded to his seat in the Senate chamber.

Vice President Joe Biden called the Senate to order. When the morning preliminary opening ceremonies were concluded, he announced, "We will be going on our August recess in the morning. Today will conclude the summer session of Congress."

Senator Williams only speaks for the final day of the summer session and served the need for the joint select committee working on spending cuts to be careful not to cut Social Security or military retirement pay benefits. He had stated, "I'm not for raising taxes, however, capping Social Security contributions and about $100,000 on annual pay is too low for the entertainers and professional athletes who receive millions in pay annually. If we tax them on the full amount of the professional income, we will have no Social Security short fall. Let's stop paying $2,000,000,000 weekly to fight in Afghanistan for example. We won't need to be paying for unwanted wars on the backs of our seniors and retired military." At the conclusion of the closing ceremony, Senator Williams again strapped on his ankle-holstered weapon.

CHAPTER 2

Upon arriving back in Folkston, Georgia, Robert Williams took a day of rest and reflection before returning to his duties as Commander of the Waycross Georgia Highway Patrol Post.

He looked at all the mail Penny had placed on the coffee table for him. It was quite a stack so he decided to put it off until after dark. With his senatorial duties and highway patrol duties, he had been unable to attend deacon meetings at Camp Pickney Baptist Church. He felt guilty at neglecting his church, so he went over and mowed the grass. The physical exercise and the pleasure of helping his church made him feel better. He put up the lawn mower, saw his clothes were covered with grass trimmings so he returned home and took a shower. Feeling refreshed, he again sat down to sort through the mail. But his mind was still on the U.S. Senate. Setting aside the mail again, he worked on the speech for the Senate floor. In it he covered the need for solar power, wind power, and hydraulic power to generate electricity. He was convinced that these alternative sources of power would cut our reliance on foreign oil.

He also looked at the garbage can overflowing and thought about the use of trash burning to generate electricity. This would slow down the need for more landfills while producing energy. The burning paper products could heat steam boilers to turn the generator.

Robert's mind wandered to the Bible classes he taught at the D. Ray James Prison. His absence in Washington had caused him to neglect these classes, too. Robert thought about his previous capture of the escapees Tim Payne and Toby Howard.

Robert picked up the telephone and dialed the warden's office at the prison. "Warden, this is Captain Williams of the Georgia patrol. I've been out of town so I have missed my Bible study classes for the past month. When I picked up the two escapees before my trip to Washington, I decided to invite Tim Payne and Toby Howard to those classes. Would you see that my class is rescheduled for next week and invite all inmates, but particularly those two?"

The warden replied, "I know Toby Howard won't be there. He was smoking illegally on the second story catwalk. When the guard approached, he slapped the cigarette in his mouth and bolted over the rail dropping to the first floor and breaking his heel bone. He's in the infirmary this week, but as soon as he gets out he is going to solitary confinement as punishment. Tim Payne is still in solitary confinement, as that was his third weapons charge when he took the guns. I don't know when I'll let him out. You'll have to conduct your Bible study without those two fellows. Sorry!"

Robert mused, "I need to put those two on the prayer chain at church."

After disposing of the third class mail, Robert stacked the bills and personal letters in one stack and threw the rest in the trash and then emptied the overflowing trash can to the outside trash container. Then placing a new garbage bag in the previously overflowing kitchen can, he felt virtuous.

Next he picked up the phone, called the Waycross post and asked for his wife Penny. When she picked up, Captain Williams said, "Hello Darling," in an imitation of deceased country singer Conway Twitty. Captain Williams continued, "I'm back, Penny, from the murder capital of the country. I only had to defend myself twice, once on the Senate floor and once in the mall park. I'm sure glad to be back in Georgia. I've missed you. Let's eat out tonight, somewhere nice."

"GREAT! Can I pick?" Penny answered with a smile in her voice.

Being married for many years, Robert knew 'if mama ain't happy, ain't no body happy,' so he responded, "Yes my love. Anywhere you can get us reservations. Some linen tablecloths would be nice. I've been spoiled at the senate dining room."

After supper, the reunited senator and his wife Penny returned home to Folkston, Georgia, thirty miles south of the patrol office in Waycross.

As Penny got out of her patrol uniform, Robert resumed work on his bible study class preparations. Then they sat in the den and enjoyed being togther

CHAPTER 3

The next day, Captain Williams returned to his desk at the Waycross Georgia Highway patrol post.

He hadn't had time to get used to his new responsibilities, yet. His mind reflected back to the six women in the five-seat Impala convertible and the subsequent stopping of the prison bus. He realized that when you are under extreme stress such as approaching those two armed fellows on that bus, that the world slows down. Everything becomes so vivid. He can remember the blue cloudless sky. How they dodge emblem appeared on the back left fender of the bus near the tail light and again the wording 'D. Ray James Prison' down the side and again that bright 'Dodge' emblem on the front fender gleamed in that hot July sun. He could remember every action from pumping the shotgun shells and blowing out the back tires of the prison bus so it couldn't drive off. It was all so vivid in his mind. But, now it was on to his new responsibilities of this post. He stared at his inbox on his desk in disbelief. He started sorting through the mail and prioritizing his responses. On some he just jotted a note and put them in his outbox directing his number two, Ron Astro, as how to handle that particular piece of mail. The ones remaining his further study he placed in the 'pending box'.

In the background he was vaguely aware of a shift change as patrol officers entered and exited the post on a staggered basis. Also in the back of his head he could hear Penny transmitting dispatch information as she keyed the mic. Finally he got up and kneed his door closed so he could concentrate on the items in his pending box.

Captain Williams was pleased that the 2012 Ford Taurus SHO police Interceptor had been so well received by patrol post commanders throughout the state. It was an awesome vehicle. He would be glad when all the LTD's in his post had been replaced by the new model. This would take three years as they were on a three-year replacement cycle. Three years of constant use put a lot of miles on the clock. As post commander Captain Williams retained a pursuit vehicle for his use during the day and on duty drive to work and back each day, he efficiently went on duty when he entered the patrol car in his own driveway. Robert thought, "At least I have a few hours away from my desk everyday. I wonder what event will delay my trip home to Folkston tonight?"

That thought was prophetic as he and Penny worked slightly different shifts, she had her own pursuit car, too. They didn't travel in the same vehicle. If either one of them ran into trouble down US 1, there was a ready back up. This afternoon that back up would be needed.

Captain Williams picked up a phone on his desk and pushed the intercom button saying, "Penny, I'm leaving the office at this time at this time and will be in cruiser 1 southbound on US 1 at this time.

The Okefenokee fires of the summer were mostly out now. There were occasional flare-ups. When that happened, the Georgia forestry department dispatched a red fire truck. As Robert drove casually south on 1, he observed in his rearview mirror the flashing red lights of a forestry fire truck. He eased his Taurus on the grass at the right and stopped his vehicle. The fire truck with lights going and sirens blaring, swept passed him. The wind generated by the large trucks passing rocked his patrol car slightly. Taking his rearview mirror before entering the highway again, he noticed that red '55 T-Bird convertible again. Because the top was down, it was obvious that Joanne Crimson, the smoke jumper, sped by in the wake of the fire truck with her red hair tussled in the breeze. On her dashboard was a rotating red light.

Robert thought to himself, "Well that red light is a great addition from the last time I had to stop her for speeding. Now I can recognize that she is in a temporary emergency vehicle and not following pursuit. Again checking his rearview mirror, Robert entered US 1. Ahead he saw the fire truck turn right into the Ware County entrance to the Okefenokee Swamp and Wildlife Preserve. Following the fire truck the little red sports car, driven by Joanne Crimson, took the corner at a fairly high speed. Robert was close enough to hear her tires squall. This peaked his interest and he decided to see what was happening in the swamp fire. He engaged the lever for his own flashing lights and re-entered the highway following the two red vehicles ahead. His powerful strobe lights reached a mile down the road. Robert signaled a right turn and followed the fire truck and Joanne into the wildlife preserve. The speeding open convertible ahead suddenly braked as it was getting near dusk. The headlights on the crimson convertible had detected an alligator in the road.

Robert thought, "I haven't even called in to let Penny know I'm not on US 1. I'll cover that when I ask for an animal control officer."

As he got on the microphone, he observed Joanne Crimson exiting her vehicle. She was approaching the gator on foot. He thought, "What a gutsy woman. Or a crazy woman?" He wasn't sure which.

Joanne ran around the alligator and marched right on to the stopped fire truck. She was an M.D. after all and was concerned to see if there were any injuries at the fire.

Soon the gator ambled off the road to the other side. Doctor Crimson then realized she was too quick to leave her vehicle and return to it and proceed to the fire.

Meanwhile, Robert informed Penny as dispatcher of his location and presumably late arrival at home. He informed her as dispatcher, that his 20 or location would be the Okefenokee Swamp and he would be late for supper.

As he drove down the entrance to the swamp fire, he spotted where the fire truck had stopped.

There was that red Impala convertible. Robert thought, "What is this a reunion? There's that smoke jumping librarian, Suzanne, again. As he approached the collection of vehicles, a forestry department helicopter descended with red lights flashing and landed in the center of the road. The perky smoke-jumping librarian jumped into the helicopter and was whisked off as she strapped on her parachute.

CHAPTER 4

The helicopter pilot was Chase Freedom. He was a former Marine helicopter pilot in Iraq. He had been working as a helicopter pilot for the Georgia Forestry Service for the past two years.

In that time he had occasion to transport Miss Suzanne _____ on four occasions. They greet each other with a friendly nod and little conversation. Chase did say, "Are your parachute straps adjusted comfortable? Do you need my help buckling your safety harness on?"

Suzanne responded with a 'click, click, click,' she said, "Everything just clicked into place.

No problem, Chase. Let's get this show on the road."

Chase responded by pulling up on the collective and the helicopter rose smoothly into the air stopping at 100 feet high. Then Chase pushed the hand control stick and foot petal simultaneously and smoothly headed the helicopter toward the rising smoke, to the southwest.

Pointing with his free hand he told smokejumper Suzanne, "It's a small blaze broken out again, you should be able to put out the fire with your fire extinguisher." In less than five minutes, Chase was flaring out the helicopter so Suzanne would not have to parachute out. Chase said, "This is a really small blaze, but we want to put it out before it spreads. I thought I would put you down close to the fire so you wouldn't have to repack your chute later."

Suzanne responded with a smile, "I am disappointed, I was looking forward to the jump. My goodness it is started to flare up again from the wind of the rotor blades." With this Suzanne jumped spritely out of the helicopter and landed on the spongy earth beneath her feet. Now she understood why the Indian word Okefenokee meant trembling earth.

Suzanne squirted her flame retardant on the fire from her hand held fire extinguisher, quietly extinguishing the blaze. She climbed back into the helicopter and swiftly strapped her self in. As the bubble-fronted helicopter arose, she had an excellent view of the ground below. When she raised her eyes to look ahead she had a panoramic view of the massive swamp to the west. Chase reversed the helicopter and soon was headed back to the fire truck. Suzanne told Chase, "I haven't jumped in the last two years riding with you. You always put me down to the fire. I need to renew my parachuting experience. If you take me up 3,000 feet, I will make a jump." At 3,000 feet Chase leveled the copter off and told Suzanne, "Go ahead and make your jump."

Suzanne unbuckled her safety harness and pushed off to the right falling face down away from the rotors. When she safely cleared the helicopter, she went from head down position to a free fall position, which slowed her descent. With two arms and two legs out it rapidly slowed her fall. She reached for the ripcord and the chute in her backpack deployed. As a graduate of the University of South Carolina in Columbia, she had 'Gamecock' on her chute. She ascended proficiently and using the guide straps to direct her to the target zone, about 100 feet from the fire truck. As a little breeze was blowing, she gathered her parachute in her arms and stuffed it into the backpack. She would replace it properly later.

Having enjoyed her first skydive in a while, she was beaming with pride as she dropped her backpack into the backseat of her convertible. She unfastened the Velcro straps on the calf of her leg holding the small fire extinguisher and placed it carefully in the floorboard in the backseat of her convertible. Waving goodbye to her fellow fire fighters, she started back to Waycross. As she looked up Chase was flaring out his helicopter for his landing to bid his fellow firefighters a goodbye; then he flew home for the evening.

After leaving the swamp and national wildlife preserve, Captain Williams stopped at US 1, signaled a right turn to head south to Folkston. Before he could pull out, he waited on a rapidly approaching 18-wheeler. When it blew by, the wind currents generated by this refrigerated truck shook his patrol car. Captain Williams knew the truck was moving way too fast. He reached over, flipped on his red and blue flashing lights and engaged the siren. The 365 horsepower motor rapidly propelled him to 80 mph but the truck sped on ahead.

Robert engaged his radar unit. The truck was doing 90 mph at that time so he showered down on his Interceptor. In no time he passed 100 mph and was soon closing in on the 18-wheeler. He saw the truck begin to slow and pull off the road, so he pulled in behind it. He left his emergency lights still rotating as he exited the vehicle. He engaged his shoulder mic and reported the situation at the dispatcher on duty in Waycross.

Touching his hand reassuringly on the grip of his Glock service weapon, he approached the driver's door cautiously. When the driver became visible, he discovered it was a woman. She had lowered her driver's window and held her CDL license up in her left hand. Robert took it with his left hand and examined it while keeping an eye on her. He read, 'Brenda Freedom'.

Captain Williams said, "You were just clocked at 90 mph in a 70 mph zone. What's the hurry?"

Brenda responded, "Officer, I've got a load of perishables, fruit and vegetables headed for the cruise ship, 'Sovereign of the Seas' at port Canaveral. They have a three hour turn around to head back to the Bahamas. In that three hours, they've got to replenish the diesel tank, unload about 10,000 suitcases, and about 2,500 passengers. In the same time they load about 50 tons of fresh fruits and vegetables and the next 10,000 suitcases and 2,500 passengers. Officer, you've got the ticket pad and you've got the gun, and I've got a load of fresh vegetables that have to be on that ship. Now either write me a ticket or shoot me, but let me go, I've got to be in Port Canaveral right now."

Captain Williams responded, "I don't know what you are going to do in Florida, but you're going to obey the speed limit in Georgia for the next hour. You're not going to kill Georgia citizens on my watch. I'm writing you a warning, but will follow you all the way the 60 miles to the Florida line. If you speed we will go back to the courthouse at Folkston where the warning will be followed by an official ticket and you can meet with the judge. You may go now, but obey the traffic laws of Georgia as you head south to Florida, I'll be right behind you."

Brenda took the warning ticket with all the courtesy she could muster at that time. She signaled her entry to US 1, checked her mirror, and double clutching, put the 18-wheeler through it's 12 forward gears. She did hold it down to the speed limit through Folkston and down to the St. Mary's river bridge. As she crossed the bridge, she again resumed the high speed necessary to reach Port Canaveral on time. As she glanced in the rearview mirror, she saw her own reflection and could almost swear that was smoke coming out of her own ears, but she knew it was from the cigarette dangling from her lips. As she pulled onto I-10 and double clutched through the 12 gears, she got back up to 90 mph. Her radar detector went off so she backed down to the speed limit. Brenda decided the fastest way to Port Canaveral was not through traffic court. As she reached Jacksonville on I-10, she followed 295 around to 95 South. Obeying the speed limit, she reached the ship on time. She thought to herself, "Life is too short, not to take one of these cruises, I'll just take my vacation week to go to the Bahamas myself."

CHAPTER 5

Captain Williams returned to the Waycross post, exited his pursuit car, and re-entered his office. The dispatcher commented, "There is an urgent message on your desk, Captain. It just came on the phone lines from Washington D.C."

Captain Williams opened the door to his office and noticed the pink telephone message sitting on his desk. It read, "You are needed urgently back in the senate for a vote on the debt ceiling limit. Please call your senate office as soon as possible."

Robert sat down in his chair, picked up the telephone, and dialed the 'Sam Rayburn Senate Office Building'.

He informed the republican leadership that he would leave immediately for Washington D.C. This time it would be necessary to fly. He hit the intercom button, called Ron Astro to take over his responsibilities at the Waycross post as he was headed to Washington. Next he called Delta Airlines in Jacksonville on his personal cell phone and got the next flight out and reserved his seat. Hitting the memory button on his cell phone, he dialed his home in Folkston and asked Penny to pack him a bag. Re-entering the Taurus, he headed down US 1 to his home in Folkston. There he met Penny at the door and she handed him his bag. Exchanging a quick kiss, he got in his F150 pick up and drove the 40 miles to the Jacksonville airport.

Arriving in Washington, he again registered at the Watergate Hotel then took a cab to the Senate office building. He was quickly briefed by the Senate Republican leadership on the upcoming votes. Back on the senate floor Senator Williams resumed his seat and listened to the ongoing debate.

As the debate raged on, Senator Williams began organizing his thoughts for some pertinent comments.

Pushing the button on his desk, indicating a desire to be recognized, Senator Williams awaited his turn. Once recognized, he rose to his feet and addressed the chamber, "Mr. Vice President, fellow senators, I'm against raising the debt ceiling limit, without corresponding cuts immediately on our spending. Republicans and democrats alike are guilty of fiscal irresponsibility. The United States Congress controls the purse strings of this nation. We are currently spending 150% of what we take in. We cannot continue to spend more than we take in. We must form a bipartisan committee to meet with a bipartisan committee of the house to begin the process of spending less than we take in. We can start by cutting our foreign aid to the 50 or so nations that we currently give billions to. Most of them don't even like us. We can't buy friendship. Next, we need to cut the size of the federal government under the Obama administration the size of the federal work force has mushroomed. We can't go on like this. The white house continues to hire bureaucrats to make up rules for small and large business to follow. These rules are expensive for US employers to meet. They are shipping our jobs overseas in many cases to avoid these expensive rules.

"It's time to give American business some relief so they can compete in the world market place. We need to cut back on the welfare society that is creating a situation where it costs people to work. Many have learned that it's better to draw welfare checks, food stamps, unemployment, and other benefits, than it is to work for a living."

Senator Williams then yielded the balance of his time to the senior senator from Georgia.

This newest senator was exhausted from a half day on patrol back in Georgia, a long flight to Reagan National Airport, and a hurried trip to get check in the motel and onto the senate floor. He was exhausted, and sat in his leather senator's chair with an audible sigh. He thought, "I sure will be glad when Dr. Astro is recovered sufficiently from her childbirth to resume her seat on the senate floor."

But it was not to be very soon. Georgia's newest senator stood to offer many alternatives to the current direction that the United States Government was taking.

In various debates, Senator Williams argued to bring our troops home from Afghanistan, Iraq, and other Middle Eastern war zones. He argued that the money could be better spent at home. He argued in favor of alternative sources of energy. He promoted the use of wind power, solar power, the generating of electricity by the burning of trash to heat water and to steam generate electricity.

Senator Williams argued against spending $2,000,000,000 a week fighting in Afghanistan when this money could be used to rebuild our nation's infrastructure such as our aging bridges and our inadequate power grid. He argued for less reliance on foreign oil. Two options he suggested were the development of alternative fuel vehicles, such as hydrogen fuel cell car. He thought 2 billion dollars a week could build a lot of needed things here at home. One suggestion he made was a monorail system down the center median of our interstate road system. He wanted to see some branch lines off the interstate to bring small towns onto the monorail grid.

Senator Williams had argued that we no longer could afford to police the world. He had argued we were only 6% of the world's population, yet we tried to police the other 94%.

In his final arguments on this day, Senator Williams said, "We have got to live within our budget. We can't continue to spend 150% of what we take in. Our credit rating has been down graded from AAA to AA+ for the first time in our history. The stock market has responded with extreme volatility. The stock market was on a roller coaster ride causing much uncertainty in the financial market place.

Senator Williams decided to call Dr. Linda Astro at the close of Senate debate today.

After checking out, picking up his ankle holster, he walked to the Senator Russell office building. Greeting his staff, he asked for a phone call to be placed to Dr. Astro at her home in Waycross. When he had Linda on the line, Robert said, "How soon will you be able to come back? This is very stressful, doing two jobs. One in Washington, and my real job back in Waycross. Now I understand how hard it was in the early days of this country. It took two or three months to get from President Jackson's home in Nashville to Washington. Obviously, he made the trip only a couple of times in a four-year period. I'm stressed out here with the speed of air travel or the use of an interstate highway. I'm ready to hand this job back to you, Senator Astro."

"Now Robert, just hang in there a little longer. I should be back soon." Dr. Astro said.

"I need to get back to my 'real job' soon." Robert continued. He went on, "This job of representing the people through elected officials was designed back in 1789 when the constitution was adopted, to be a part time job, not a permanent job."

"Elected officials seem to think that a congressional position is lifetime employment. They vote to give themselves raises, huge benefits, huge staffs to do the work, free postage, free overseas trips or so called 'junkets', and on the list goes! We need to cut the size of the government. One place to start would be the senate staff."

Dr. Astro replied, "Now Robert, you're preaching to the choir. I agree. I happen to be an appointed senator filling out a term, just as you are an appointed senator for the time of my maternity leave. Neither of us is a member of the Washington establishment. We didn't raise money in a campaign for office. We don't owe our votes to any special interest contributors. Please hold out another week or two, and I'll be back." Linda responded with her college professor voice.

Robert sighed and said, "Pshaw, I guess this Georgia boy can hold on that long. I look forward to your early return. Thanks Linda. How's Ron holding up doing his job and mine too?"

Linda responded, "He's about as ready for you to come home as you are to get here. He's doing two jobs, too. He's just not having to commute back and forth to D.C."

Robert thought, "I can hold out a while longer, by going home for a few days to check on Penny and the situation at the Waycross post."

This he did.

I hope you have enjoyed my official portrayal of our current situation in Washington, D.C. For all our government's faults, it's still the best government in the world. We will overcome these difficulties portrayed in this personal account. Each generation needs to learn from the history of those who preceded them. We can't take our freedoms and way of life for granted. We must continue to do our best and pray for our leaders. We need to be informed voters in selecting those who represent us in Washington.

Dr. Carl R. Stekelenburg
LaGrange, Georgia
August 2011

BACK COVER

Officer Robert Williams gets his Master's Degree in Criminal Justice and is quickly promoted from road duties to command duties with a rank of Captain. He is placed in command of the Waycross, Georgia patrol post.

His assistant is Ron Astro. Ron's wife is Dr. Linda Astro, professor of political science at Waycross College. Governor Nathan Deal had the responsibility of appointing a new U.S. Senator upon the death by heart attack of the existing junior senator. Officers Ron and Robert had both performed courteous service for the governor and his protection detail on his visits to Waycross.

The previous year they and their wives, Dr. Linda and Penny, had attended a governor's ball and fundraising dinner at Waycross College. The governor had been impressed with both couples. He was particularly impressed with the economic and political understanding of both Dr. Linda and Robert.

When the junior senator died of a heart attack, the governor, already acquainted with Dr. Linda Astro, quickly appointed her to fill the remaining term of that senator as provided by state law. Linda quickly accepted, but didn't mention she was three weeks pregnant. Off to Washington D.C. she went. She represented Georgia quite well, but the child continued to grow within her. Soon she was forced to seek maternity leave. Governor Deal had to appoint someone on a temporary basis while Dr. Linda was in the hospital. This was just too important a time for Georgia not to have two senators in Washington. President Obama was pushing for an increase in the debt ceiling for the current budget year of 2011. He had already shoved down Georgia's throat the Obama health care plan. Governor Deal immediately thought of Officer Williams to fill the post temporarily while Dr. Linda was in the hospital.

Officer Williams requested and was granted extended leave without pay to temporarily become a U.S. Senator.

This book is his story.

This is Dr. Stekelenburg's sixth book. His five previous books are: "High Plains Cowboy", "Blind Date", "The Burton Murder and other short stories", "Gunfight at Dutchman's Well", and "Canadian Cowgirl".